Max
the Brave

by Ed Vere

PUFFIN

This is Max.

Doesn't Max look sweet!

Max looks so sweet that sometimes
people dress him up in ribbons.

Max does **not** like being
dressed up in ribbons.

Because Max is a fearless kitten.

Max is a brave kitten.

Max is a kitten who chases **mice**.

Max the Brave just needs to find out
what a mouse looks like . . .

and then he will chase it.

Maybe Mouse is in there.

Max bravely explores the can.
'Mouse? Are you in?'

Hmmm, Mouse isn't here.

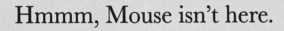

Oh, hello . . .

'Are **you** Mouse?'

'No, I'm Fly,' says Fly. 'But I just saw
Mouse scurry by a moment ago.'

Hmmm, maybe this is
what Mouse looks like.

'Excuse me, please,
but are **you** Mouse?'

'I'm not Mouse, I'm Fish,' says Fish.
'But I just saw Mouse dash outside.'

That **must** be Mouse,
up in the tree.

'Excuse me, please, but are **you** Mouse?'

'We are not Mouse, we
are birds,' say the birds.

'But we did just see Mouse scoot by.'

'Excuse me, but would **you**
happen to be Mouse?'

'Eeek, Mouse?!
I'm not Mouse, I'm Elephant,'
says Elephant.
'But I did just see Mouse skitter by.'

'Thank you very much,'

says Max.

'And **you**?'

'Nope . . . thattaway.'

'Hello there. Are **you** Mouse by any chance?'

'Who, **me**? No, certainly not,
I'm Monster!'
squeaks Mouse. 'But I did just see
Mouse asleep over there . . .

If you're very quick, you might catch him.'

'Thank you very much,' says Max.

This **must** be Mouse.

Hmmm, I didn't know Mouse was so BIG.

'Ahem, excuse me, **Mouse**, will you wake up please?

I am Max the Brave,

and I have come to chase **you**.'

'Wakey, wakey, Mouse!'

yells Max as he bounces up and down
on Monster's head.

'I am Max the Brave and I chase mice!
And I might just eat you up too!'

Hmmm, I didn't know Mouse had such BIG teeth.

GULP!

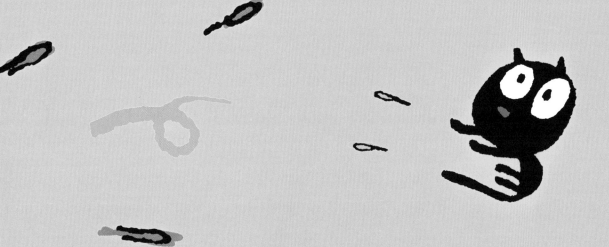

'Yuk!'

Max decides that chasing mice
is not all it's cracked up to be.

And anyway, he doesn't need to be
Max the Brave all the time . . .

Unless he's out chasing . . .

. . . monsters.

for
gatita

PUFFIN BOOKS
UK | USA | Canada | Ireland | Australia
India | New Zealand | South Africa
Puffin Books is part of the Penguin Random House group of companies
whose addresses can be found at global.penguinrandomhouse.com.
www.puffinbooks.com
First published 2014
This BookTrust edition published 2017
003
Text and illustrations copyright © Ed Vere, 2014
The moral right of the author/illustrator has been asserted
Made and printed in China
A CIP catalogue record for this book is available from the British Library
ISBN: 978–0–241–33570–3
www.edvere.com   @ed_vere